For my sweet sisters—
Sandra Fergins, who hardly talks at all,
and Marcia Shelf, who fills in the silences.
Love, A.S.M.

To Pamela
S.V.

THIS STORY IS BASED ON A TALE
FROM ACCRA IN GHANA, WEST AFRICA.

First published 1995 by Walker Books Ltd
87 Vauxhall Walk, London SE11 5HJ

2 4 6 8 10 9 7 5 3 1

Text © 1995 Angela Shelf Medearis
Illustrations © 1995 Stefano Vitale

This book has been typeset in Maiandra GD.

Printed in Hong Kong

British Library Cataloguing in Publication Data
A catalogue record for this book
is available from the British Library.

ISBN 0-7445-4013-5

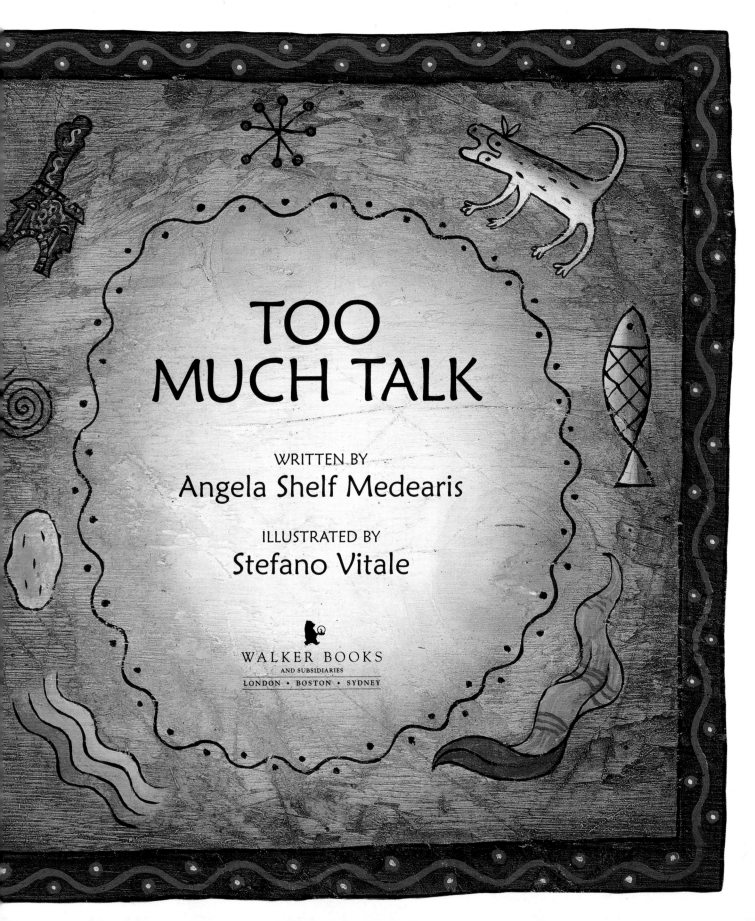

TOO
MUCH TALK

WRITTEN BY
Angela Shelf Medearis

ILLUSTRATED BY
Stefano Vitale

WALKER BOOKS
AND SUBSIDIARIES
LONDON · BOSTON · SYDNEY

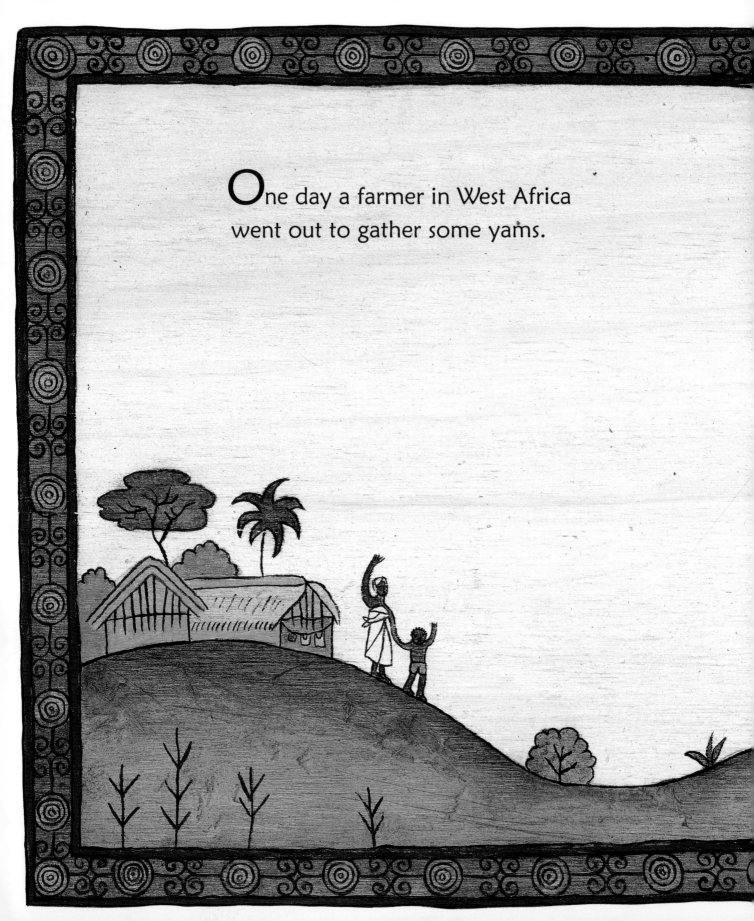

One day a farmer in West Africa
went out to gather some yams.

While he was digging, a yam said to him, "You did not water me. You did not weed me. And here you come to dig me up!"

"Well!" said the farmer. First he looked around. Then he looked at his dog and said, "Were you talking to me?"

"No," barked the dog. "It was the yam."

"Aiyeee!" screamed the farmer. He ran and he ran, uphill and downhill. And he ran and he ran, downhill and uphill. He ran until he met a man who was carrying some fish.

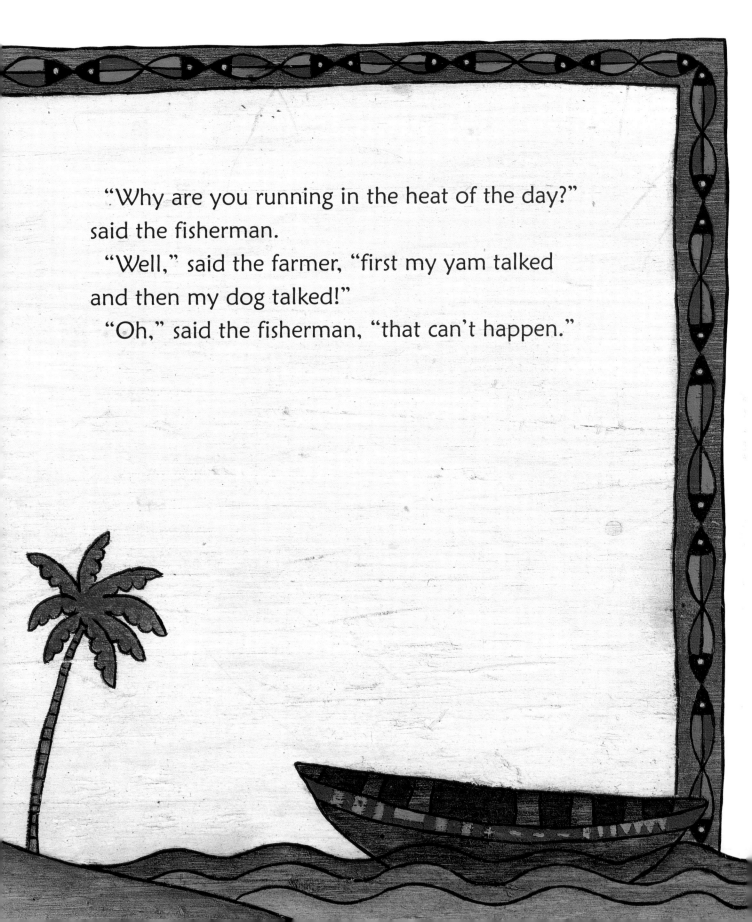

"Why are you running in the heat of the day?" said the fisherman.

"Well," said the farmer, "first my yam talked and then my dog talked!"

"Oh," said the fisherman, "that can't happen."

"Oh, yes it can," the fish said to them. "Aiyeee!" screamed the farmer and the fisherman. They ran and they ran, uphill and downhill. And they ran and they ran, downhill and uphill. They ran until they met a man who was weaving some cloth.

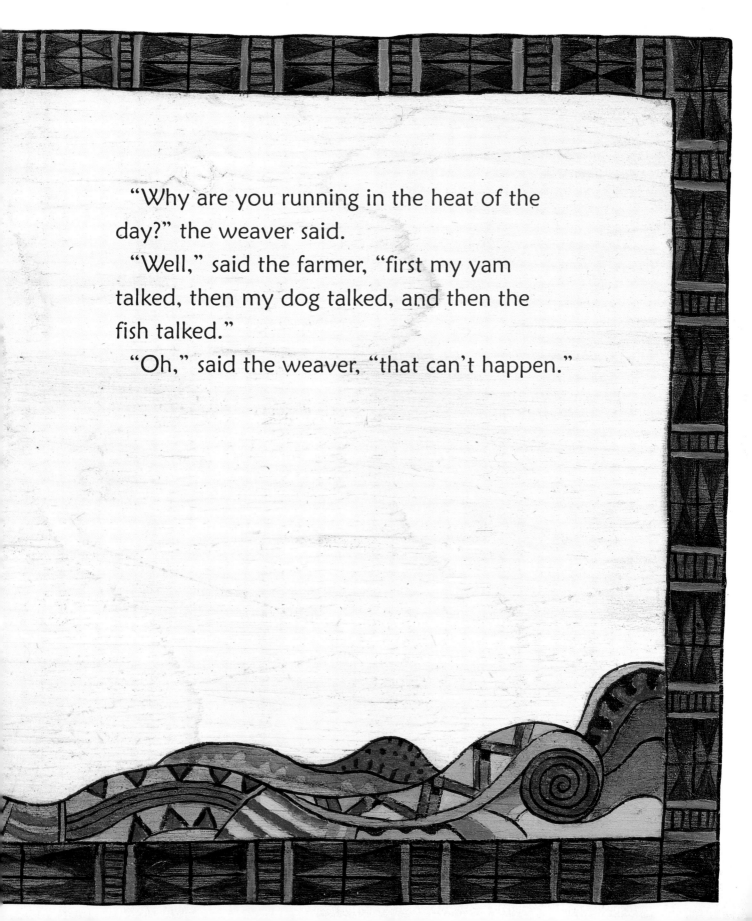

"Why are you running in the heat of the day?" the weaver said.

"Well," said the farmer, "first my yam talked, then my dog talked, and then the fish talked."

"Oh," said the weaver, "that can't happen."

"Oh, yes it can," the cloth said to them. "Aiyeee!" screamed the farmer and the fisherman and the weaver. They ran and they ran, uphill and downhill. And they ran and they ran, downhill and uphill. They ran until they came to a woman who was swimming.

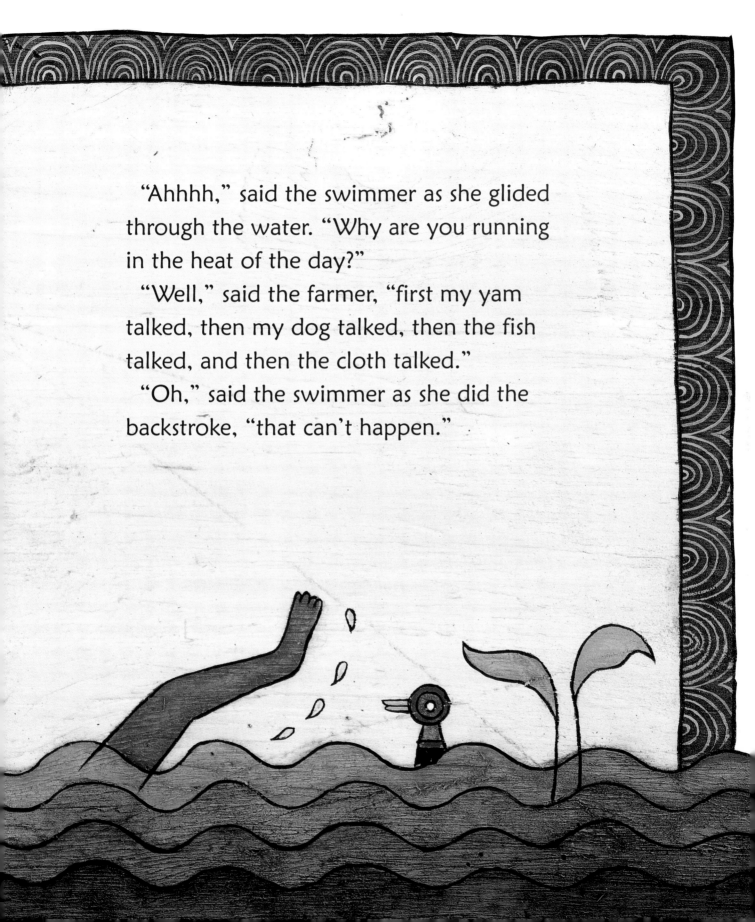

"Ahhhh," said the swimmer as she glided
through the water. "Why are you running
in the heat of the day?"

"Well," said the farmer, "first my yam
talked, then my dog talked, then the fish
talked, and then the cloth talked."

"Oh," said the swimmer as she did the
backstroke, "that can't happen."

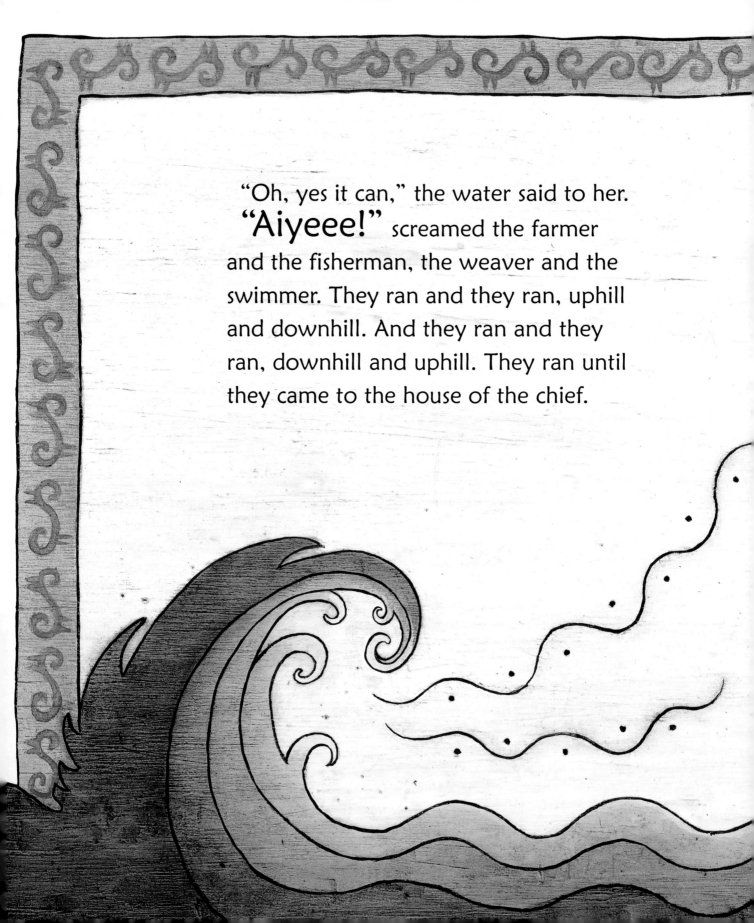

"Oh, yes it can," the water said to her. "Aiyeee!" screamed the farmer and the fisherman, the weaver and the swimmer. They ran and they ran, uphill and downhill. And they ran and they ran, downhill and uphill. They ran until they came to the house of the chief.

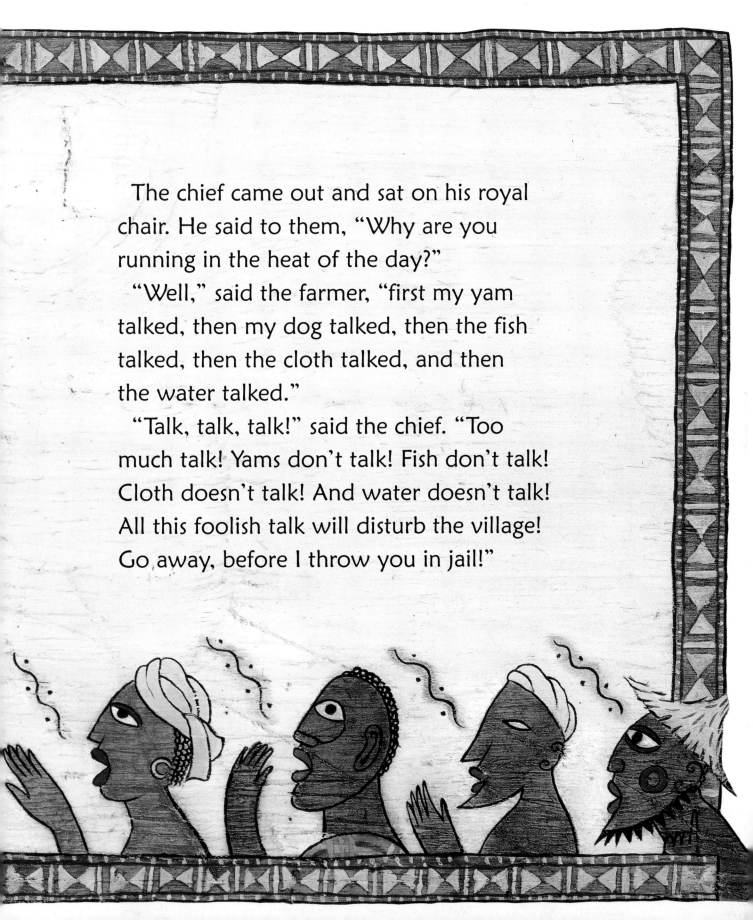

The chief came out and sat on his royal
chair. He said to them, "Why are you
running in the heat of the day?"

"Well," said the farmer, "first my yam
talked, then my dog talked, then the fish
talked, then the cloth talked, and then
the water talked."

"Talk, talk, talk!" said the chief. "Too
much talk! Yams don't talk! Fish don't talk!
Cloth doesn't talk! And water doesn't talk!
All this foolish talk will disturb the village!
Go away, before I throw you in jail!"

So they all ran away.

"Imagine," said the chief, "a talking yam! How can that be?"

"So true," said the chair. "Whoever heard of a talking yam?"

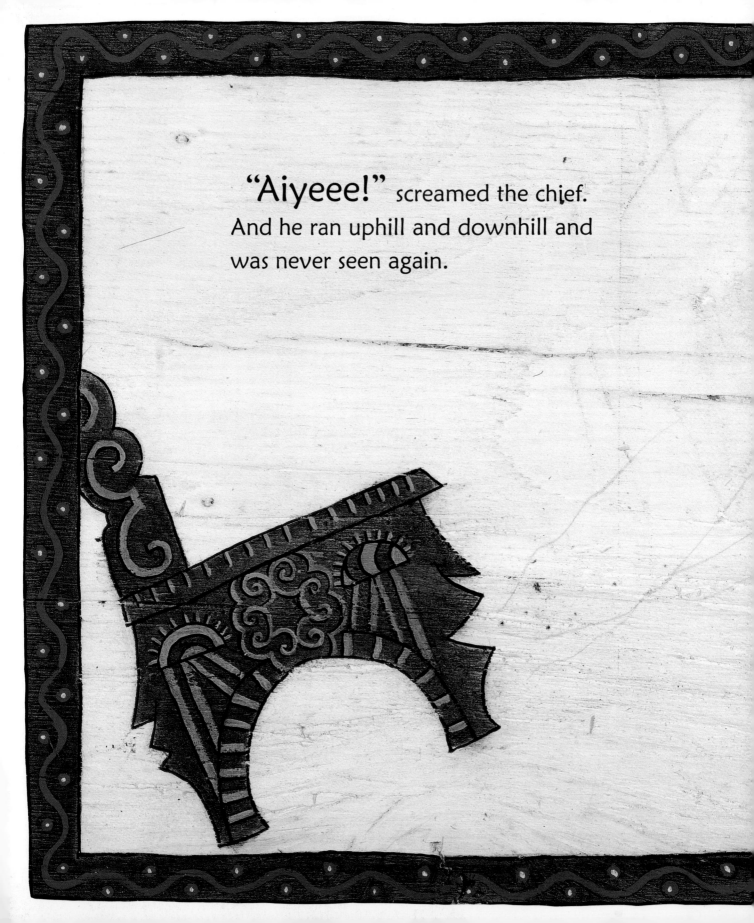

"Aiyeee!" screamed the chief.
And he ran uphill and downhill and
was never seen again.